DOG
TO THE RESCUE II

SEVENTEEN
MORE
TRUE TALES OF
DOG HEROISM

JEANNETTE SANDERSON

AN
APPLE
PAPERBACK

SCHOLASTIC INC.
New York Toronto London Auckland Sydney

For Vee and Leo Soricelli

Photo Credits

Bear: Chazz Sutphen; **Bo, Champ and Buddy, Reona, Sheena, Willy, Woodie:** Heinz Pet Products; **Boomer:** Teri Smith; **Chelsea:** Catherine Pound; **King:** Fern Carlson; **Klutz:** Lisa Funderburk; **Lady:** *Reporter Herald*, New Hampshire; **Papillon:** Ron & Mindy Wynne; **Poudre:** *Greeley Tribune*; **Shadow:** Chris Ackerman/*Boston Herald*; **Silver:** Athena Lethcoe; **Tribber:** Susan Pattman.

No part of this publication may be reproduced in whole or in part, or stored in a retrieval system, or transmitted in any form or by any means, electronic, mechanical, photocopying, recording, or otherwise, without written permission of the publisher. For information regarding permission, write to Scholastic Inc., 555 Broadway, New York, NY 10012.

ISBN 0-590-48573-3

Copyright © 1995 by Jeannette Sanderson.
All rights reserved. Published by Scholastic Inc.
APPLE PAPERBACKS is a registered trademark of Scholastic Inc.

12 11 10 9 8 7 6 5 4 3 2 1   5 6 7 8 9/9 0/0

Printed in the U.S.A.   40

First Scholastic printing, September 1995

Acknowledgments

It is impossible to thank all the people who helped me write this book, but I would like to attempt to do just that.

I would like to thank all those who shared their wonderful stories with me — Fern Carlson, Tina Cavacco, Marvin Dacur, Lisa Funderburk, Donna Holzworth, Athena Lethcoe, Laura Martinez, Susan Pattman, Missy Perkins, Catherine Pound, John Rayner, Anneliese Schmidt, Betty Souder, Ray Thomas, Dale Windsor, and Ron Wynne.

I would also like to thank the many other people from around the country who helped me collect and research these stories. In particular, Judi Braudy at the Mt. Vernon, NY, Public Library; Dominique Davis at the American Kennel Club Library; Melissa Bassett of the Massachusetts Society for the Prevention of Cruelty to Animals; Kay Clark of the American Humane Association; Kevin Conroy of the United States Police Canine Association; Barbara Koon and Doreen LePage of the American Rottweiler Club; Kris Provenzano, editor of *Smooth Colliers*; Dianne Spessard of the Potomac Boxer Club; Terry Thistlethwaite, editor of *Collie Connection*; and Jessie Vicha for the Quaker Oats Company.

I would like to thank librarians around the country — including those at the Field Library in Peekskill, NY; the Cleveland, OH, Public Library; the *Rutland Herald* Library; and the *Loveland Daily Reporter-Herald* Library — for making my work easier by doing their jobs so well.

I would also like to thank my editor, Dona Smith, for her kindness and patience. I would like to thank my husband, Glenn, for patiently listening to and reading countless dog stories, my three-year-old, Catie, for making me repeat each story so often that I learned the best way to tell it, and my baby, Nolan, for leaving me enough energy to write these stories. Thanks to Maria Johnson and Danielle Clarkin for keeping Catie and Nolan safe and happy while I worked. And thanks to Patsy Sanderson, Alice Sherman-Quine, and Helen O'Reilly for their support.

My thanks to the person or persons I must have left out.

And, finally, my thanks to brave dogs everywhere — and to these seventeen dogs in particular — for giving us stories to tell.

Contents

Bear

Four-year-old Zeke toppled backward into the icy water. He couldn't get his balance, and his wet clothes and water-filled boots were starting to weigh him down. His two sisters frantically tried to help from shore, but they couldn't find a branch long enough to reach him. It looked as if the start of the children's Christmas vacation was about to end in tragedy. Then Bear, the family's big black dog, leapt to the rescue.

Like many farmers, the Perkinses were having a problem keeping their small livestock alive. The ducks and chickens that should have been food for the New Haven, Vermont, family's table were instead being devoured by raccoons, foxes, and weasels.

"We felt like a dog was the only thing that would take care of that problem," Missy Perkins says.

The family was living on a very tight budget, so when Missy saw an ad for a free three-year-old mongrel that had outgrown its owner's apartment, she thought she'd found the answer to her prayers. But when the dog's owner brought the shaggy beast by the farm the next day, Missy wasn't so sure.

The dog was half-Newfoundland, a breed that can grow up to weigh as much as 150 pounds. Missy figured the owners must have known she was going to be a big dog. Was there another reason they were giving her away?

"I worried that maybe there was something wrong with her," Missy says.

Missy's misgivings were quickly overruled by her five children's instant delight with the dog. They just fell in love with her. In the end, Missy agreed to keep the dog as long as she could return her if she gave them any trouble.

The dog's former owners had called her Rosie.

"We didn't think she looked anything like a Rosie," Missy says. "And the last thing she smelled like was a rose. We thought she looked like a giant bear, so that's what we called her, Bear."

The big black dog fit right in at the farm. She watched over the small livestock. She also watched over the Perkinses' children.

Bear was especially vigilant around water. For centuries, her Newfoundland ancestors had helped Atlantic Coast fishermen rescue drowning men. Bear was going to see to it that none of her charges drowned. She swam circles around the children when they went for a dip in the river, and she barked if she thought they swam too far from shore.

On December 19, 1987, Bear's water-rescue abilities were truly put to the test. It was a Saturday, the first day of Christmas vacation. Martha, eight, Sarah, seven, and Zeke, four, were playing with Bear in the snow. They decided they wanted to go sliding on one of the ponds, and asked their dad if it was okay. Dale Perkins knew that the two small ponds on their property had frozen almost to the bottom during the recent cold spell. He figured they'd be safe sliding around there and told the children to go ahead. Then he went inside the house.

The children and Bear ran to the first pond and slid back and forth across the ice. It wasn't long before Sarah announced that she was bored.

"Let's go to Lee's Pond," she said.

Their neighbor Lee had a pond, about 250 yards from the Perkinses' farmhouse and hidden by a row of trees, that was bigger than their own. Wouldn't it be a lot more fun to slide there? Martha and Zeke readily agreed and the trio headed to Lee's Pond, with Bear by their side.

The children never questioned whether or not the ice on Lee's Pond was frozen enough to slide on. After all, their own ponds had been frozen solid. Wouldn't Lee's Pond be frozen solid, too?

Sarah, Martha, Zeke — and even Bear — skidded joyfully onto their neighbor's pond. Zigzagging across this 70-foot-wide pond *was* a lot more fun than sliding on their own. So much fun, in fact, that they soon tired themselves out. The children sat down on the ice to rest, and their 80-pound dog lay beside them.

But their combined weight was too much for the ice to bear. It cracked and gave way, plunging the three children and their dog into the icy water. Bear quickly leapt to shore. Martha and Sarah, who were near the edge of the pond, managed to grab hold of trees to pull themselves to shore. Zeke wasn't so lucky. The four-year-old, who was farthest from shore, was too small to reach one of the lifesaving tree limbs.

Zeke tried to stand but couldn't. The water was only about two feet deep, but the pond's bottom was muddy and crowded with briar bushes. It was impossible for the boy to get his footing. Zeke kept falling backward, into deeper and deeper water. And all the while his soaked clothes and water-filled boots were getting heavier and heavier, threatening to weigh him down and pull him under.

Martha and Sarah screamed for help and frantically looked for a branch long enough to reach their brother, who was moving farther and farther away from them.

When Bear realized what was happening, she

plunged back into the icy waters to rescue Zeke. The dog locked her powerful jaws on the collar of the boy's jacket, then dragged the frightened child to a place where he could stand. Then she let go of Zeke's jacket, walked in front of the boy, and offered him her tail. Zeke grabbed hold of it, and the dog towed him to shore.

That's where Missy found her three cold, wet, frightened children just minutes later. She had heard their screams and, terrified of what she'd find, ran down there as fast as she could. She hugged Martha, Sarah, and Zeke while Bear licked their cold, tear-stained faces.

The story of Bear's rescue spread quickly. A California animal-rights group heard it and awarded Bear a gold cup and a red, white, and blue ribbon. And, of course, the Perkinses gave her lots of extra love and attention that Christmas.

The episode taught Missy Perkins that Bear was an "incredibly intelligent" dog.

Zeke learned something that day, too.

"I learned never to go anywhere without the Bear," the four-year-old told his mom. Missy says she had hoped for something along the lines of "I learned to ask permission before I do something." But she didn't mind. After all, she figured, Zeke couldn't go too far astray with Bear by his side.

Bo

Bo went for a swim nearly every day in the Roaring Fork River near his home. Rob and Laurie Roberts didn't know just how strong a swimmer their nine-month-old black Labrador retriever had become until their raft overturned in the fast-moving rapids of the Colorado River, trapping Bo and Laurie underneath it.

It was a beautiful Sunday in June, and Rob and Laurie Roberts decided to do what they often did on warm, sunny mornings — ride the rapids of the Colorado River. They drove to Maintenance Rapids, just east of their home in Glenwood Springs, Colorado, and set their rubber raft in the water. Then they climbed in, along with their two puppies, nine-month-old Bo and three-month-old Dutchess, for another exciting adventure.

Shortly after they shoved off, their adventure turned into a nightmare. An eight-foot wave came crashing down on them and flipped their raft. Rob and Dutchess were thrown clear downstream to safety. But Laurie and Bo were trapped underneath the boat.

Rob tried to swim upstream to save his wife. But the current was too strong. So he had to wait, frightened and helpless, and hope that his wife would be able to escape from under the raft.

Minutes passed. Water sprayed from beside the raft. And up shot Bo, alone. Rob was afraid he had lost his wife. Then Bo dove right back under the raft. Seconds later the dog re-emerged, pulling Laurie by the hair. Once free of the raft, Laurie grabbed Bo's tail. The dog then used his powerful legs to tow his mistress across the strong current to shore.

Laurie was exhausted from her ordeal. She had swallowed a lot of water. Boulders along the river bottom had left her scratched and bruised. And Laurie's head hurt where Bo had grabbed her by the hair during his underwater rescue. But all of that was nothing compared to the fact that she was alive.

"I felt I was going to drown," she said. "If it weren't for Bo, I know I wouldn't be alive today."

That night, the Robertses awarded Bo a large steak dinner.

The following year, Ken-L Ration awarded the heroic puppy its gold medal for canine courage, naming Bo the 1982 Dog Hero of the Year.

Boomer

Tina Cavacco was getting ready to feed her cats and dogs one morning when a big black bear showed up for breakfast. Before Tina and her animals could become part of the bear's morning meal, her dog, Boomer, leapt to the rescue.

Most mornings Tina Cavacco of Altoona, Florida, goes out to her carport to feed her cats and dogs. This Wednesday morning in May, 1993, was no different. The animals sat and waited, while Tina leaned on a bench and cut ham off the bone left over from the boiled dinner she'd made the night before.

It was quiet at the edge of the Ocala National Forest where Tina lived. Quiet, that is, except for the four cats and four dogs begging for their breakfast. Tina had just about finished cutting the ham when the noises her animals were making suddenly changed. She turned to see what was the matter and came face-to-face with a bear. Tina screamed and the bear stood up on its hind legs.

"He was a black bear, about five-and-a-half feet tall at least — and big," she remembers. "He was only a few feet away from me. I looked him right in the eyes."

Tina froze in terror. Most of her animals seemed to do the same — except for her boxer/pit bull, Boomer. The one-and-a-half-year-old dog she had rescued from a local humane society just months before wasn't going to let anyone hurt his mistress — or steal his breakfast. Boomer leapt through the air and grabbed the bear by the neck. Then he started shaking and shaking him.

The bear was startled, but he fought back. His claws ripped into the brave dog's head. Boomer was bleeding, but he kept fighting. His owner looked on in horror.

"I was going crazy, screaming, throwing things, trying to break them up," Tina says. She never thought of running in the door behind her. "My dog is getting killed right in front of my face," she remembers thinking. But she wasn't worried only about her dog. "I thought, there's no one for nearly one hundred acres. If this bear wins, who knows if he's going to take all of us on?"

Tina threw plants, water bowls, and food dishes at the bear. Within minutes, she had nearly emptied her whole carport. She was still screaming, when suddenly the bear just bolted. Boomer dropped to the ground.

"I thought he was dead," Tina says.

Tina ran and lifted her 50-pound hero who, though bleeding from several head wounds, was miraculously still alive. She put him in the car, then locked the other animals in the house, in case the bear came back. Then she got in her car and rushed Boomer to the vet.

The doctor washed Boomer's wounds. He gave the dog several shots to try to prevent infection. Then he sent him home. "He's in rough condition," the doctor said, "but I think he'll make it."

By that afternoon, Tina wasn't so sure.

"He was messing," Tina says. "He couldn't even get up to go the bathroom. That really scared me."

Also, Boomer's face had swelled so much that one of his eyes seemed to disappear. Tina was afraid that her dog would go blind in one eye. Then, when the swelling finally started to go down, Tina noticed a big growth in the dog's throat. It was an abscess, an infection where one of Boomer's wounds had been. The vet had to cut the abscess out, and Boomer had to have a hose in his neck to drain the infected fluids.

Tina is sure that the bear would have killed Boomer if it hadn't been so startled. It came upon a human, four dogs, and four cats, when all it expected was a ham breakfast.

"I really didn't want to see the bear get hurt," Tina says. But still, she's glad Boomer did what he did. "I think he protected all of us," she said. "He's my hero."

The people at the Orlando Humane Society think so, too. They gave Boomer a medal for his heroism.

That bear was the first bear Tina had ever seen. She also hopes it's the last. But just in case, she's keeping her protector nearby.

"I'm not going out without Boomer by my side," she says.

Champ and Buddy

Most people would consider two dogs barking in the middle of the night a nuisance. But for Marvin Dacur, who was trapped under a 2,680-pound tire in a freezing-cold warehouse, the dogs' barking was his only hope.

It was 12:45 A.M. on Friday, December 13, 1985, and Marvin Dacur wasn't feeling very lucky. He had just pulled his semitrailer into the warehouse in Dickinson, North Dakota, with two huge tires to unload. And it looked as if he was going to have to unload them alone.

Usually, one of the other truckers driving the same route would have stopped to help. But Dacur had been delayed five hours when he made the pickup, so the other truckers were all long gone. Dacur called someone who worked at the warehouse during the day to ask if he would come down to help, but he wouldn't. Dacur then called his dispatcher to tell him about the situation. The

12

dispatcher just told him to do the best he could.

Dacur braced himself against the cold — the temperature was 25 degrees below zero without the windchill — and climbed up onto the trailer. Then he began trying to move the 2,680-pound tires. With a diameter of 93 inches, it towered over him. Dacur rolled the tire a little ways and let it fall against the side of the trailer. Then he stood it back up, pushed it, and let it fall again. He did this until he got the tire to the end of the trailer.

As Dacur pushed the tire off the truck, it hit the warehouse overhang. This made the tire wobble back and forth. Dacur, having jumped off the truck along with the tire, attempted to steady it, but he was no match for the huge tire. Before he knew what was happening, the tire started to lean toward him. Dacur tried to jump out of the way, but he couldn't. The tire hit him on the right shoulder, knocked him down, and dropped on his right leg, pinning him to the cold cement floor.

Pain tore through Dacur's body. He grimaced as he lifted his head and saw his right leg — from above his knee down to his foot — underneath the tire. His ankle was twisted so that he could see the bottom of his cowboy boot.

The tire was too heavy to allow Dacur to free himself. But where could he get help? The warehouse workers wouldn't be there until nine o'clock the next morning. That was seven hours away.

Dacur shivered, as much from fear as from the cold. It wasn't even a question of having to cope with the pain all that time. Unless he got help soon, he would surely freeze to death.

Dacur began shouting for help and pounding on an overhead door. He didn't expect anyone to hear him at that hour, but there was nothing else he could do.

Meanwhile, Anneliese and Harvey Schmidt were wondering what was wrong with Champ and Buddy. Their two dogs wouldn't stop barking. A truck had pulled into the warehouse across the street a short while ago, but the dogs should have been used to that. Trucks pulled in and out of there all the time, at all hours.

Mrs. Schmidt decided to let the dogs out. She knew they wouldn't stay out for long; they never did when it was this cold. Anyway, she figured, once they realize this truck is just like any other, they'll come back in, quietly.

But that didn't happen. Once they got outside, Champ and Buddy just kept barking and barking. Mrs. Schmidt called them several times, but they refused to come in. Buddy, a mixed breed, stayed near the house. But Champ, a Cairn terrier, stood at the end of the long driveway, near the street, and barked.

Across the street, Marvin Dacur heard the dogs and knew they were his only hope. He kept pounding on the door, shouting, and making as much noise as he could. He had to keep those dogs barking. Then maybe someone would come out and see what was going on.

Mrs. Schmidt was sure the dogs were going to wake all the neighbors. She quickly put on her housecoat to go out after them.

When she got outside, all Mrs. Schmidt heard was the dogs barking. She hurried down the long driveway and was about to grab Champ by the collar when she heard something else. It was a man calling for help. And it was coming from the warehouse across the street.

Mrs. Schmidt rushed back to the house to tell her husband that there was someone in the warehouse hollering for help, and he'd better go see what was going on. Mr. Schmidt quickly dressed and ran across the street.

When Mr. Schmidt found Dacur, he wasn't sure how he was going to lift that heavy tire off his leg. He grabbed a two-by-four in the corner of the building and tried lifting the tire with that. He managed to lift the tire several inches before the piece of wood broke and the tire came crashing back down on Dacur's leg.

Mr. Schmidt looked around again. He rolled a pallet jack over and wedged one corner of it underneath the tire. Then he jacked the tire up off Dacur's leg. Dacur, wincing in pain, reached down with his hand, grabbed his boot, and dragged it out from under the tire.

By the time Schmidt got Dacur to the hospital, blood was pouring out of Dacur's right boot. Emergency room doctors immediately cut the boot off. Two bones were sticking out of Dacur's leg — one at the ankle and the other about four or five inches above it. Dacur had suffered a compound fracture of the ankle and severe injuries to his knee. Doctors operated on his leg for four hours.

After the accident, Marvin Dacur could no longer drive a truck; but he could walk and, most important, he was alive. Doctors told Dacur that if Champ and Buddy hadn't been so persistent, he would have frozen to death.

The lifesaving dogs became instant celebrities. They were written about in newspapers and magazines all around the country. They made several national television appearances. And they won Ken-L Ration's 1986 Dog Hero of the Year award, becoming the first pair ever to share that honor.

Chelsea

When Catherine Pound came to, her dog Chelsea was drooling on her face and licking her head. The Chesapeake Bay retriever wasn't just being affectionate. She was saving her owner's life.

It was a hot summer night in Fort Worth, Texas. Catherine Pound had just been out working with Merlin, her male Chesapeake Bay retriever, to prepare him for an upcoming dog show. Now Chelsea, her female Chesapeake, was barking and scratching at the front door to let Mrs. Pound know she wanted her turn. It was late and Chelsea didn't need a workout, but Mrs. Pound decided to take her out anyway. She always gave her dogs lots of attention.

Once outside, Chelsea took off at a trot down the street. Mrs. Pound held the dog's leash and ran by her side. They hadn't gotten far from home when Mrs. Pound caught her right foot in a shallow hole in the street.

17

"It was just about one-inch deep," Mrs. Pound says. But it was enough to throw the woman way off balance. "I remember the sensation of flying through the air," she says. But when she slammed into the road, she blacked out. She was unconscious for about 20 minutes. When she came to, Chelsea was drooling on her face and licking her head. Mrs. Pound wondered what the dog was doing. She had not yet realized that she was hurt.

Then Mrs. Pound reached up to touch her head where Chelsea had licked it. It was sticky with blood, but it was no longer bleeding. That wasn't the case with her elbow and knee. "The fall tore all the way through my new thick blue jeans," says Mrs. Pound.

She tried to stand but couldn't. As she lay bleeding on the asphalt, she knew she had to get help. The chances of someone finding her on this quiet street at this hour were slim.

Her only hope was Chelsea. She unhooked Chelsea from her leash so she would go home. But the dog stood over her and refused to leave.

Mrs. Pound knew then that she would have to go with Chelsea. But she would need Chelsea's help in getting home — and finding it. Mrs. Pound could no longer remember where she lived.

The injured woman grabbed hold of Chelsea between her shoulder blades. The dog took over from there. She dragged her mistress past three houses, up the walkway of a fourth, and onto the front porch. By then Mrs. Pound recognized where she was — home. She reached up and rang the doorbell. Then she lay on the porch and waited for her husband to come out.

When a doctor examined Mrs. Pound, he told her that Chelsea may have saved her life. Chelsea wasn't just being affectionate when she drooled over her mistress's head and licked her temple. She was acting like a four-footed paramedic and stopping the blood that was pouring from the gash in her head. The doctor said there was no telling how much more blood Mrs. Pound would have lost if Chelsea hadn't sealed the wound.

"There was already a tremendous amount of blood down my neck and in my hair," Mrs. Pound remembers. "I imagine it was pumping pretty hard."

But Chelsea did more than seal the wound. She also cleaned the dirt and gravel out of it. She did such a good job, in fact, that Mrs. Pound has no scar on her head from the fall. She does have scars on her elbow and knee, however.

"It's amazing that there's no scarring on my head," Mrs. Pound says.

Mrs. Pound is full of wonder and gratitude. "There's no telling what would have happened if Chelsea hadn't done what she did."

King

King didn't seem like much of a present when the Carlsons found him lying on their doorstep late one Christmas Eve. He had a gaping, infected gunshot wound in his head. And he appeared to be half-starved to death. But King went on to prove that you can't judge a gift by its wrapping when he saved the family from a devastating house fire five years later.

"Is that what I think it is?" Fern Carlson asked her husband Howard late one Christmas Eve as they returned to their home in Granite Falls, Washington, after visiting friends and relatives. She was pointing to a big, dark object lying in front of their sliding glass doors. It looked like a dog.

"I think it is," he said.

"I'm taking the kids in the front way," she said. "Get rid of it."

The Carlsons' old family dog had recently died of a heart attack, and the two children had been heartbroken. Mrs. Carlson didn't want another dog. She didn't want her kids to suffer that type of loss again.

After Mrs. Carlson got her children in bed, she went into the kitchen. Her husband told her, "He's been shot. It's all infected, and it looks like he's half-starved to death. What do you want me to do?"

Mrs. Carlson looked at the clock. It was nearly midnight. She knew there was no way they would be able to get hold of a vet at this hour on Christmas Eve.

"Well, bring him in," she said. "We'll see what we can do."

Mrs. Carlson went to the medicine cabinet to see what she could find. She came back with a bottle of hydrogen peroxide. She looked at the dog her husband had just put down on the kitchen floor. He was a big dog — half German shepherd and half Alaskan husky — and obviously hurting. The skin in his skull was laid open where a bullet had passed through his head.

"The only thing I've got is peroxide," Mrs. Carlson said. "If you want to try to hold him, I'll pour it on him."

Mrs. Carlson started to pour the peroxide into the dog's wound.

"He seemed to know we were trying to help him," Mrs. Carlson says. "I know it had to burn, and he crouched as if it hurt. But at the same time he never tried to bite us, he never growled; he just let us do it."

After pouring on the peroxide, the Carlsons fed the dog. Then they went to bed. Mrs. Carlson remembers telling her husband, "We'll get him to a vet. But no more dogs. I'm not going to listen to those kids howl about losing their pet again."

They took the dog to the vet the next day. The doctor gave the animal — who he figured was about two years old — some medicine to help clear up the infection. Then the Carlsons took him back home until he was well enough to give away. After about two weeks, when the dog's condition had improved, Mr. Carlson approached his wife.

"When do you want me to get rid of him?" he asked.

She looked at him in disbelief.

"Get rid of who?" Mrs. Carlson asked.

They had the dog for another 17 years.

King, as the Carlsons called him after their old dog, proved his worth on many occasions. But he became a true hero on Christmas night, 1981.

The Carlsons had had company that day. When the last of the guests left some time after ten o'clock, the family went to bed. The bedrooms were at one end of the house, the family room was at the other. King slept in the family room, where the sliding glass doors were left open for him to get as much cool, fresh air as he wanted. A ply-

22

wood door separated the family room from the laundry room, and King from the rest of the house.

About four hours after the family went to bed, a fire broke out in the laundry room. King could have run right out the open sliding glass doors to safety, but he didn't. He chose to save the family that saved him.

King clawed and chewed at the closed plywood door until he made a hole big enough to squeeze through. Then he bolted through the burning laundry room, through the kitchen where the fire had started to spread, and through the living room into 15-year-old Pearl Carlson's bedroom. There he began pulling at the sleeping girl.

"Get out of here," the teen said sleepily. When he wouldn't stop, she sat up to push the dog away. That's when she noticed her room was filled with smoke.

Pearl ran down the hallway to her parents' bedroom, with King at her side.

"Wake up!" she hollered. "There's smoke everywhere!"

Mr. and Mrs. Carlson jumped out of bed. Mrs. Carlson looked worriedly at her husband, who had a bad lung.

"Get out of here!" she yelled at him.

As soon as she said that, Pearl panicked and ran out of the bedroom and back toward the living room. King ran after her.

"You get out," Mrs. Carlson told her husband. "I'll get Pearl out." Then she took off toward the living room to find Pearl.

"I grabbed Pearl and got her back to her bedroom," Mrs. Carlson recalls. "It wasn't as smoky at that end of the house. I got her out her bedroom window and then tried to get King out." But King refused to leave the house. "He kept turning on me and running back toward our bedroom."

"Do you see your dad out there?" Mrs. Carlson asked Pearl.

"No," she said. "I can't see nothin' out here."

"Well, don't you come back in," Mrs. Carlson told her daughter. "I'm going to find him."

Mrs. Carlson ran back into her bedroom. By now smoke had filled the room. She couldn't see anything. Then she felt King by her side. She reached down and grabbed his collar. King pulled her to where her husband was lying on the bedroom floor. He had stopped to try to save something from the fire and been overcome with smoke.

Mrs. Carlson knew she couldn't get her husband out alone. She managed to rouse him enough so that he could put one arm around her and one arm around King. Then she and the dog dragged Mr. Carlson back to Pearl's bedroom. There, Mrs. Carlson shoved and Pearl pulled Mr. Carlson out the window.

Once he made it outside, Mr. Carlson collapsed.

Mrs. Carlson knew they had to get him away from the burning house. She sent Pearl to the nearest neighbor — who lived about five acres away — to call the fire department and get help.

When the neighbor appeared, he and Mrs. Carlson carried the unconscious man down to the road.

"To get to the road," recalls Mrs. Carlson, "we had to walk by our bedroom. I looked in and our bed was on fire."

The fire department arrived within minutes, but it was too late to save the house. Luckily, its occupants had survived, relatively unharmed.

King, however, wasn't in great shape. A firefighter noticed that the dog's fur and paws had been badly burned. The pads on his paws had been so scorched that it would be more than a year before he could walk on hot pavement.

When someone tried to feed the four-footed hero a sandwich and King refused, Mrs. Carlson's brother looked inside King's mouth. It was full of splinters. That's when the Carlsons realized that King had chewed through the door to save them. (King had to have all those splinters removed before he could eat again.)

And for the rest of his life King had a spot — as Mrs. Carlson describes, "about as big and round as a silver dollar" — where the fur never grew back on his neck.

"I don't know if that's where his dog tags were, whether they got so hot and burned him, or whether something got hot and fell on him," she says.

And no one knows for sure what caused the devastating fire, although Mrs. Carlson suspects a faulty microwave oven.

One thing that they do know for sure, however, is that King saved their lives.

"King was the best Christmas present we ever received," Mrs. Carlson says. "That dog was a hero. There's no way we would have gotten out. In the first place, we probably wouldn't have woken up." (The Carlsons' electric smoke alarm was useless given the electrical failure caused by the fire.) "Second, I couldn't have found Howard in all that smoke and I'd have probably ended up passing out from it. And I wouldn't have had the strength to get my husband out; not without King's help."

The Carlsons weren't the only people who considered King a hero. The dog was written about in dozens of newspaper and magazine articles. The story was even on a national TV show. Finally, King was named Ken-L Ration's 1981 Dog Hero of the Year.

Klutz

Klutz didn't look like much of a hero. In fact, the beagle-dachshund mix got his name after tumbling down the stairs on his stubby legs and knocking a glass of milk into a bowl of spaghetti. "What a klutz!" everyone said. But that's not what people called the 28-pound dog 11 years later. When Klutz attacked a five-and-a-half-foot rattlesnake to protect his owner's three-year-old daughter, people called him a hero.

Lisa Funderburk, her three-year-old daughter Lyndsey, and her mother were in the kitchen eating lunch. Klutz, Lisa's 11-year-old beagle-dachshund mix, was sunning himself just outside the back door of Lisa's parents' home in Lehigh Acres, Florida. Lyndsey finished her lunch ahead of her mother and grandmother and decided to go to the back door and call Klutz.

No one can say for certain what happened next. It appears that when Lyndsey opened the door,

Klutz, who had always been protective of the girl and her mother, panicked. There was a giant rattlesnake within easy striking distance, and Klutz must have feared that the toddler was going to come outside. Klutz didn't wait for Lyndsey's next move. He did what the dog must have felt he had to do. He attacked the rattler before the snake could attack Lyndsey.

Within moments, Lisa heard Klutz yelping and carrying on. She jumped up from the table and ran to the back door.

"I could hear the rattle," she remembers. "It was so loud and echoed so much that I couldn't tell where the snake was."

Klutz was lying on the ground. But not for long. He quickly got back up and headed toward the snake, which Lisa now saw for the first time.

"I've never seen a snake that big," she says. "When he was coiled and had his head up, he was as big around as my legs — and I'm not a light person."

Lisa screamed for Klutz to get back, but the dog ignored her. Lisa knew she had to get her dog. She couldn't go out the back way — the snake was in her path. So she ran out the front door and around the house. By the time she got out back, Klutz was staggering. But he was trying to go back after the snake. Lisa quickly picked him up, threw him in the car, and sped to the nearest vet's office, which was two miles away.

"The whole way I was just crying and screaming," Lisa remembers. "I told him, 'You can't die. It's Christmastime. I already bought your gifts.' "

By the time they reached the vet, Klutz was having convulsions and foaming at the mouth.

"Please, please save my dog," Lisa begged.

The vet looked at Klutz. His prognosis wasn't good. Klutz had been bitten above both eyes, and the fang marks were four inches apart. The doctor told Lisa he had seen cows and horses die from fang marks that were just two inches apart. This snake must have been a lot bigger — and more poisonous — than those deadly snakes. In addition, Klutz wasn't a young dog. The doctor really didn't think he'd make it. And trying to save him would be expensive.

"I don't care how much it costs!" Lisa said. "Just save my dog."

The vet gave Klutz two shots of antivenin at $200 apiece. That was December 18, 1990.

Klutz stayed at the vet for six days. Each day Lisa would visit him and stay until she had to go to work. She never brought Lyndsey, because she didn't want her daughter to see Klutz in such bad shape. The dog's head was grotesquely swollen and he could barely open his eyes. Lisa did, however, bring all sorts of treats from home, including her mother's homemade spaghetti and meatballs.

"Klutz was always on diet dog food because he was so puny and his back used to kind of cave in when he gained weight," Lisa says. "But when he was at the vet's, my mother said, 'Forget the diet dog food. Feed him and he'll get better.' "

By Christmas Eve, it appeared that the antivenin and homemade cooking were working their magic. Klutz could stand a little bit, and the swelling had gone down. The vet let Lisa take Klutz home.

Lisa took the dog home to a warm family welcome. Lyndsey was thrilled to see her lifesaver. Klutz seemed glad to see her. But within hours, Klutz's condition began to worsen.

"It was as if he had come home to see Lyndsey and make sure she was okay before he died," Lisa says.

By Christmas morning, Klutz was struggling to breathe. Lisa called the vet at home. He said to bring Klutz to his office. After examining him, the vet said Klutz was having complications from the antivenin and would need a blood transfusion.

The vet gave Klutz the transfusion, and the dog seemed to be doing better. But the doctor stayed with him all Christmas day and slept by his side that night to watch over him, just in case.

Lisa got a call at six o'clock the next morning. It was the vet. Klutz had died at four o'clock that morning.

Lisa was sorry to have lost her hero, but glad to have her daughter. If Lyndsey had been bitten instead of Klutz, the snake probably would have killed her. She and Klutz weighed the same — 28 pounds — but the human hospital was a lot farther away than the vet's office.

Lisa has lots of mementos of Klutz. One is the rattles cut from the deadly snake. The number of rattles show that the snake was about 11 years old, the same age as Klutz — and an age Lyndsey will now see, thanks to her brave dog.

Lady

Lady is "the most nonaggressive, lazy dog you've ever seen," says her owner. In other words, Lady is not the type of dog you'd expect to be a hero. But that's just what she is. The husky-retriever mix earned herself a new reputation when she leapt into a den of rattlesnakes to save the life of eight-year-old Teresa Martinez.

It was Labor Day, 1992, and Laura Martinez and her extended family were doing what lots of families across America were doing — they were roasting hot dogs. Theirs wasn't a backyard barbecue, however. The roast was on some undeveloped land the family owned.

When the children said they had to go to the bathroom, their grandmother led them to the only sheltered area on the big grassy field — a small bank of about ten pine trees. Eight-year-old Teresa Martinez ran ahead of the others. She didn't realize she had run past a den of rattlesnakes until their rattling filled the air. When she turned around and looked, there were five or six rattlesnakes between her and her grandmother. Teresa screamed.

"Stand still," her grandmother said.

Laura Martinez, Teresa's mother, was about 25 feet away at the barbecue site when she heard her daughter cry, "Oh my, I'm scared. Come and get me!"

Laura ran to help Teresa, but Lady, the family's nine-year-old husky-retriever mix, beat her to it.

"Lady took off when she heard Teresa scream, even though she had been exhausted by the long walk from the car," Laura said. "She got right in there for the kids."

Lady attacked the snakes and kept them distracted enough to allow Teresa to run to her mother. Laura Martinez got Teresa and all the other children into the car and then ran back to get Lady.

Laura called Lady but the dog refused to retreat until she looked around and made sure all the children were safe. Then Lady walked over to her mistress and collapsed at her feet.

At first, Laura didn't think Lady had been bitten. Teresa told her otherwise. Laura loaded the dog into the car and rushed to a neighbor's house to call the vet.

"Don't bring her here," the vet told Laura. "There's nothing we can do. Take Lady to Colorado State University Veterinary Teaching Hospital in Fort Collins."

Lady's head was beginning to swell. Laura got some ice to put on it. Then she headed for the hospital, which was about 20 miles away.

"By the time we got there, her face had swollen to twice its usual size," Laura says. "You couldn't even find one eye. It had swollen shut."

The vet took Lady and quickly cut off her collar, which was suffocating her. Then he examined the dog and found three bites.

"How far do you want us to go?" the vet asked.

"You need to do whatever you can," Laura told him. "She's a hero. She saved a bunch of children today."

The vet then explained that the antivenin, which was expensive, could cause complications. And Lady wasn't a puppy anymore. Her age wouldn't help her recovery.

Laura didn't care what the antivenin cost. They had to try to save Lady. She said she wanted to go ahead with the treatment. The vet didn't have any antivenin on hand, and had to send for it from Poudre Valley Hospital (antivenin is also used for humans), which was about ten miles away. Laura drove to pick it up, to keep things moving along.

After the vet gave Lady two vials of the medicine, he told Laura to go home. Lady's fate would be decided in the next 24 to 36 hours, he told her.

"Monday night was pretty traumatic," Laura recalls. When she called the hospital at nine o'clock the next morning, she didn't know what to expect. She was pleasantly surprised.

"Lady's doing great," the vet told her. "You can pick her up this afternoon."

It was lucky for Lady that she felt better than she looked.

"She looked awful," Laura says. "Her face was shaved, bruised, and swollen. But it was the best reunion."

During the next week or so Lady spent most of her time sleeping.

"The vet said that was pretty much to be expected with snake bites," Laura said.

When she was awake, though, Lady got extra special treatment — hot dogs with her medicine. And she got lots of praise from her owners.

"We all just feel like Lady's an absolute hero," Laura said. "Lady is the most nonaggressive, lazy dog you've ever seen," she says. But that day she was totally the opposite. "She just laid down her life to save us," her owner says. "We're just really grateful to her."

Lady got lots of extra attention from outside the family, too. Her bravery was written about in newspapers. She was a runner-up in Ken-L

Ration's 1992 Dog Hero of the Year contest and won the New Hampshire Doberman Rescue League's unsung hero award. This award is usually reserved for Doberman pinschers, but the League made an exception for Lady, because of her outstanding bravery.

Papillon

Papillon paid so much attention to the new baby that Ron and Mindy Wynne thought he must be jealous. The couple even talked about giving the two-year-old collie away. But when the baby was just five weeks old and Papillon saved her life, the Wynnes' outlook changed. They realized that they had mistaken the collie's natural protectiveness for jealousy. And they knew they wouldn't give Pappy away for the world.

Mindy Wynne fell in love with a collie at the pet store in the Salem, Ohio, mall where she worked. She kept telling her husband how much she wanted it, but he didn't seem to pay much attention. So she just kept visiting it during her work breaks and hoping that one day it would be hers.

Then one day when Mindy went to play with the dog, it was gone.

"Where's my collie?" Mindy asked.

"It's been sold," the pet store employee told her.

Mindy was heartbroken, but not for long. When she got home from work, she discovered that the dog had been sold to her husband. Mindy named the beautiful long-haired collie Papillon, after the breed in the cage next to him at the pet store, and looked forward to many happy years with this new family member.

But two years later, the Wynnes feared that they couldn't keep Pappy much longer. Although the dog got along well with their nine-year-old, Amanda, and their seven-year-old, Matthew, the couple was worried about how he was behaving around their newborn, Rachel.

"He acted what we thought was very, very jealous when Rachel was born," Ron says. "He was always right there, right where the baby was."

Ron and Mindy were concerned for the baby.

"We thought all the attention Papillon was giving the baby was jealousy," Ron says. "We thought maybe we ought to get rid of him."

All that changed on June 19, 1993. Mindy fed five-week-old Rachel a bottle of formula and then put her in for her nap. While the baby slept peacefully on her back, Mindy went to take a shower.

Mindy had just gotten in the shower when Pappy started barking wildly. Afraid he was going to wake the baby, Mindy called through the closed bathroom door for him to be quiet.

"He's a very well-trained dog," Ron says. "But he wouldn't shut up."

Before Mindy could try to quiet him again, Papillon slammed into the bathroom door, knocking it off its hinges. The powerful dog then jumped into the shower and back out again. Mindy sensed trouble and followed him.

"He ran around, barking, knocking doors open, and finally burst into the baby's room," Mindy says. "He jumped up and put his front paws on the crib. . . . When I looked at the baby, she was blue." Rachel had stopped breathing.

Mindy screamed, then immediately started doing cardiopulmonary resuscitation (CPR) to revive her infant. Amanda, who had been playing in the yard when she heard her mother scream, ran in to see what was happening. When she saw her mother performing CPR, she called 911. An ambulance arrived minutes later and rushed Rachel to the hospital.

Rachel, who is fine thanks to Papillon, had suffered from something called reflux. While Rachel was sleeping, she spit up some of her food and it went back down the wrong way. Instead of going down her esophagus, it went down her airway, stopping her breathing. If Papillon hadn't been so insistent in alerting Mindy to Rachel's condition, the baby would have choked to death within minutes.

"We're just real pleased and real proud," says

Ron. "We're just tickled pink with Papillon."

And what of the talk about giving him away? "I don't see that as a possibility anymore," Ron says. "He's staying right here."

Papillon has become a local and a national hero. He was grand marshall of a parade in the Wynnes' hometown of Trotwood, Ohio, and was named first runner-up in Ken-L Ration's 1993 Dog Hero of the Year contest.

Poudre

Dale Windsor named his new golden retriever for the Poudre River, where he liked to fish. He didn't know that Poudre would one day save his life by pulling him from that river.

Dale Windsor loaded his fishing gear into his pickup and climbed behind the wheel. Poudre, his seven-year-old golden retriever, climbed in beside him. Then they headed for the Poudre River for a day of fly-fishing.

It was a warm September morning. It had rained the day before, but this day had dawned clear and sunny. Dale drove to a spot about 40 miles up the river. He parked his truck and took the equipment he thought he'd need. Then he and Poudre climbed down a steep bank to the river's edge.

Dale soon realized the fish were biting the green willy worm that day. He checked the box of flies he kept on his belt, but that one wasn't there. It was back in the pickup.

Dale scrambled back up the bank. He got the worm from the truck and turned to head back down to the river. But he was in such a hurry that he forgot the rocks were still wet and slippery from the previous day's rain. He took one step and slid on a rock. Then he tumbled all the way down the steep riverbank.

"I hit every rock and then went face first into the river," Dale remembers. He must have blacked out, because the next thing he knew he was lying faceup in the water. His head was wedged between two rocks, his feet were resting on the bank, and his dog was by his side.

Dale knew he had to get out of there right away.

"I was concerned because the water is controlled from upriver," Dale says. "There's a lake that they release periodically. If they release it, the river can go up three or four feet."

Dale twisted to try to free himself, but a bad back limited his mobility. Then he tried to use his arms to get free, but his right arm was useless. He'd shattered it trying to protect his head during the fall. In desperation, he even tried to use his feet to pull himself to shore. All he managed to do was pull his boots off.

Finally, Dale turned to Poudre, his only hope. He grabbed her collar with his left hand, and told her what to do.

EAR

BO

BOOMER

**CHAMP
AND
BUDDY**

CHELSEA

KING

KLUTZ

LADY

PAPILLON

POUDRE

REONA

SHADOW

SHEENA

SILVER

TRIBBEI

WOODIE

WILLY

"Pull me, girlie," Dale said. And that's just what Poudre did. The 100-pound dog pulled. She pulled and pulled until she got her 180-pound master close enough to shore so that he could grab hold of a rock and, with Poudre's help, haul himself onto the riverbank.

Once there, Dale tried to stand, but couldn't. His head was so banged up from the fall he was dizzy. So he got on his knees and once again grabbed hold of Poudre's collar with his left hand. Then the dog slowly dragged her master over the sharp and slippery rocks up the steep embankment.

"She was frothing at the mouth, she was pulling so hard," Dale remembers. "It was just choking her. We had to stop about five times."

When they finally made it to the pickup, Dale managed to hoist himself into the truck. Then he had to make a decision. He was 60 miles from home. He knew there was an emergency station about five miles from where he was, but he was afraid of what would happen to Poudre if he drove there and let them take him to the hospital. He was worried that there would be no one to look after the dog.

"I couldn't leave her in the hot sun in the pickup," he says. "And I couldn't just leave her on the road." Dale was afraid that she'd either get hit by a car, or be stolen.

Showing more concern for his dog than for himself, Dale began the long drive home. Since his right arm was useless, he had to use his left hand to steer. He also had to use it to reach across his body and shift gears on the standard transmission. By the end of the torturous ride, he began to black out. But somehow he made it. When he got to his house, his wife rushed him to the emergency room.

"It took three hours to put my arm back together," he says. "It's crooked now, but it works good."

Dale lost his hat, his creel, and his fly-fishing rod to the river that day. But, thanks to Poudre, he didn't lose his life.

"I was really fortunate that I had her there," Dale says. "Even the doctor said there must have been an angel with that dog."

As a result of her bravery, Poudre was named runner-up in Ken-L Ration's 1993 Dog Hero of the Year contest.

Reona

Reona's first owners abused her and tried to make her into an attack dog. But Reona was much better suited for saving people's lives than for threatening them. She proved that when she rescued a five-year-old girl during the 1989 San Francisco earthquake.

Reona hadn't had much of a life before she came to live with the Pattons. The rottweiler pup had been abused by her first owners, who wanted to make her into a guard dog.

"They'd done everything in the world to make this puppy mean," Ron Patton says.

A breeder rescued Reona from this awful home, but those months of abuse were hard for the dog to shake. When Reona joined the Patton household, she was in such bad shape that she wouldn't let her new owners near her for a week.

But the Pattons were kind and loving. And Reona — whose name is a play on the word reowned — settled happily into her new home.

One of the Pattons' neighbors was Vivian Cooper. Like many young children, five-year-old Vivian was afraid of big dogs. Reona was no exception.

All that changed on October 17, 1989, when Reona saved Vivian's life.

Vivian was in the kitchen with her mom when the earthquake hit. Jars of pickles, chocolate syrup, and mayonnaise came crashing out of the refrigerator and down on Karen Cooper. The woman broke her foot and cut her leg. Vivian started screaming.

Reona, who was several houses down, heard Vivian's screams. The two-and-a-half-year-old dog bolted out the door and jumped three fences to get to the Coopers' yard.

"I got to the door once, and the earthquake moved me back," Karen Cooper says. "That's when I thought we were going to die."

Then she looked outside and saw Reona.

"There was this big brown face," she says. "Reona looked at me as if to say, 'What is the matter with you?'"

The 102-pound dog rushed inside where Vivian stood, frozen in terror, in the middle of the kitchen. Reona pushed the terrified girl against the cabinets and sat on her. Just then, a large microwave oven on top of the refrigerator came crashing down on the spot where Vivian had been standing. If Reona hadn't knocked Vivian out of the way, the appliance surely would have killed her.

Reona saved Vivian's life in another way, too. She kept her calm. Vivian hugged Reona tightly and buried her head in the dog's fur until the shaking stopped. Vivian's mother credits Reona's presence with preventing one of Vivian's epileptic seizures, which are often triggered by excitement. Karen Cooper says that such a seizure would have been fatal at that time. Even if she had been able to reach her daughter, which she wasn't, the earthquake had scattered Vivian's medications everywhere.

"When I finally got over to Reona, I said, 'Can I have my baby, please?' " Cooper says. "And Reona looked at me like, 'Well, if you're calm enough.' " Then the brave rottweiler walked out the door.

Needless to say, Vivian is no longer afraid of Reona.

"Now there's a bond between them that just won't quit," Jim Patton says.

For her bravery, Ken-L Ration named Reona its 1989 Dog Hero of the Year.

Shadow

When 12-year-old Greg Holzworth got lost in the snow-filled woods behind his home one cold winter night, the dog that followed him everywhere became more than his "Shadow." He became his lifesaver as well.

Greg Holzworth decided to take his dog for a walk in the woods around his Raynham, Massachusetts, home. It was a bitter cold Sunday afternoon in February and the ground was covered with nearly a foot of newly fallen snow. But Greg didn't care about the weather. He had just finished writing a book report and felt he needed to get out of the house.

The sixth-grader put on a hooded sweatshirt and a denim jacket. He pulled on his mittens and laced up his boots. It was four o'clock when he and Shadow, his nine-year-old black Labrador retriever, headed out into the snow-filled woods.

Greg and Shadow often walked in the woods together. They had begun these walks when they lived in Colorado, and continued them when they moved to Massachusetts 18 months earlier. Greg never worried about getting lost. He always made a path to help him find his way out.

That day, as Greg made a fort in the snow, Shadow wandered away. When Greg heard his dog bark, he went to find him. Shadow was in a briar patch.

"When I got there he took off and I followed him," Greg says. "When I tried to follow my tracks back, they were all covered with snow."

Greg looked around him. He squinted to make out what he could in the enveloping darkness. But it was useless.

"Everything looked the same because it was swampy," Greg says. "I had no idea where I was."

When Greg hadn't returned by five o'clock, his mother and father got worried.

"I knew he wouldn't stay out when it was dark," his mother, Donna Holzworth, says. "I just kept wishing he was at a friend's house and not lost in the woods. We knew he was in trouble because Shadow didn't come home. We thought the dog would come home for help if he thought he could leave Greg there."

Donna and Donald Holzworth knew that nightfall was making it less and less likely that Greg would be able to find his way out of the woods. Donald, who was a hunter and knew his way in the woods, set out to find his son.

Donna Holzworth watched the door — and the clock. When an hour passed without a sign of her son or her husband, she called the police.

Meanwhile, Greg was becoming very cold and tired.

"I wasn't scared," he says. "I was just getting wicked cold and my legs were sore."

At one point, Greg heard his father yelling, but couldn't yell back because his throat was so sore. That's when he figured he was going to be out in the cold for a while. So he tried to establish some sort of makeshift shelter for himself in the woods.

Greg sat by a tree and cleared away the snow as best as his numb hands allowed. Then he built a wall to try to stop the assault of winds that made the temperature feel like 20 below. Finally, he tried to cover himself for warmth. But all he could think to cover himself with were branches, and his hands were too numb for him to be able to break them from the trees.

At this point, many people would have panicked. But Greg kept his wits — and his dog — about him.

"I'd heard that when people get lost they usually lie together in a group to share their body heat," Greg says. "So I pulled the dog on top of me. . . . Shadow just stayed with me the whole time."

And it was a long night. More than 100 local firefighters, police, neighbors, and other volunteers combed the woods for hours looking for the missing boy. It was slow work, searching this snow-covered area of dense woods.

"A television crew [testing the night's visibility] tried to see the house from just fifty feet into the woods," Donna Holzworth says. "They couldn't."

Hours passed. The night was so cold and wet that ice was forming on the boy and his dog.

"My legs were frozen," Greg says.

But Shadow stayed on top of him, giving Greg his body heat. At about one o'clock in the morning, Shadow gave him something else — his voice.

"I thought I heard someone calling me," Greg remembers. "But then I didn't hear it again and I figured it was just my imagination." Greg would have been unable to answer a call anyway, his throat was so raw from the cold.

But Shadow barked. He barked and he barked until someone heard him. Francis Leary, a 37-year-old Raynham resident, had heard the call for volunteers on his citizens band radio earlier that night. Leary, along with his brother Michael, a nephew, Ted Durrigan, and a friend Roger Menard, found Greg and Shadow. They wrapped their coats around Greg and called to other members of the search party that they had found him. Then, led by a searchlight from a Massachusetts State Police helicopter, they led the boy from the woods. Greg was only a half-mile from home.

Greg was rushed to nearby Morton Hospital. He was soaked to the skin and his temperature was two degrees below normal. But his injuries were so minor that less than 12 hours later he was sitting in his living room complaining only of tingling fingers and toes.

Things could have been a lot worse.

"You have to give the kid a lot of credit. He really kept his head about him," says Raynham police sergeant, James Hastings. "And you have to give Shadow a lot of credit, too. It could be that he saved that boy's life."

Greg's mother believes he did.

"I would consider Shadow a hero," she says. "His body heat is what kept Greg warm."

The people at the Massachusetts Society for the Prevention of Cruelty to Animals also think that Shadow is a hero. The humane society named him its 1990 Animal Hero for helping Greg survive the long, cold night of February 26, 1990.

Sheena

John Rayner had a bag of groceries in one hand and his cane in the other. He was about to open the trunk of his car when two men came rushing at him. One yelled, "I'll knock him down, you grab his wallet." John's only hope was Sheena. The dog whose life John had saved just six months earlier was going wild as she watched the attack from the backseat of his car. As John was spun around, he reached for the door handle and pulled it, setting Sheena free.

When John Rayner looked out in his front yard in April of 1991, he saw something strange.

"I thought it was a dead dog," the St. Petersburg, Florida, resident says. John, who had been disabled in a car accident years earlier, grabbed his cane and went out to investigate. Upon closer examination, he found that his original guess was wrong. The mass of black and brown fur was a dog. But she wasn't dead.

"She was half-dead, really," John says. "She was cut up all over. She was totally dehydrated. Her feet were filled with sandspurs."

After John gave her ice chips and a soggy face-cloth to lick, the dog gave him such a look of gratitude that it stole his heart.

"I knew when she looked at me she was mine," he says of the dog, a Belgian-shepherd mixed breed.

He also knew that the animal needed immediate medical attention. Her cuts needed to be cleansed and stitched. But she was too weak to make it to the vet. Luckily, John had once worked as a registered nurse. So he and a friend carried the dog into the kitchen. There John cleansed the wounds and gave the dog the butterfly stitches she needed. He gently removed the sharp sandspurs from her feet. Then he fed her and gave her more to drink.

Under John's expert care, the once abused dog slowly recovered. When the dog was strong enough for a trip to the vet, the doctor pronounced her in good shape. John had nursed her well. Sheena repaid John for his kindness during a shopping trip just six months later.

It was a warm fall day and John had just finished doing his weekly grocery shopping in nearby Gulf-port. He wheeled his cart out to the parking lot and there, with his cane in one hand, he lifted a bag of groceries from the shopping cart. He was about to unlock the trunk of his four-door Chevy when two men came rushing at him.

"I'll knock him down, you grab his wallet," one of them shouted.

Sheena, who had come along for the ride, had been waiting in the backseat while John went shopping. The windows were halfway down to give her air. She was excited when she saw her master returning to the car. But when she saw his attackers, she went wild.

"She started going really crazy, trying to fit through the opening of the window," John says. He knew that Sheena's door was unlocked. "I never lock that door if I have a dog in the car, in case I have to get them out quickly because of the heat down here," he says. But he didn't know how he would get to the door and open it.

As his mind raced, one of the men grabbed him by the shoulders and whipped him around. The other ripped the chain off his neck, then tried to tear the watch off his wrist.

John took his cane, which he was carrying in his right hand, threw it up in the air, and caught it by the bottom. Then he whacked one of his assailants over the head with it. The blow broke the cane's wooden handle and, more importantly, knocked one attacker to the ground, bleeding and unconscious.

"Then the other guy got very upset and really started roughing me up," John says. "He spun me around, to get my wallet, I guess."

With the spin, John was within reach of the door handle that would set Sheena free.

"I figured, all I have to do is pull and fall to the right," John says. And that's just what he did.

Sheena flew out of the car, wrapped her teeth around the assailant's neck, and knocked him to the ground.

"Don't bite," John told her.

Without Sheena's teeth holding him in place, the wiry attacker managed to squirm under the car and wriggle to the other side. Once there, he got up and ran.

Sheena, relieved of her prisoner, started licking her master. But John didn't want the man to get away.

"Go get him!" John told her. Sheena took off.

"She crossed the main boulevard, which scared me," John says. "Then I saw her take off down an alleyway." Sheena came back 10 or 15 minutes later. The assailant who had fled was nowhere in sight.

"I think she had fun," John said. "She was panting, but her tail was wagging."

John picked up his spilled groceries as best he could. He asked the supermarket manager to call an ambulance for the fallen assailant. Then he went home with his dog, his hero.

Sheena tied for first place with another dog for

Ken-L Ration's 1991 Dog Hero of the Year award. But for John Rayner, Sheena has no equal.

"I have a bond with her that I never had with any other dog," John says. "She's my special friend. We look out for each other."

Silver

Athena Lethcoe drifted in and out of consciousness. She didn't want to wake up, but something was wrong. Her dog, Silver, was nudging at her, growling, barking even. She never did that. Something clicked and Athena realized she was slipping into a diabetic coma. If she didn't eat right away, she would die. But she could barely move. How would she get upstairs to the kitchen? How would she stay awake? Her answer came in the form of a bark.

Athena Lethcoe breeds collies. She has 40 of them at her home in Nikiski, Alaska. But one of the beautiful dogs, a three-year-old smooth collie, stands out from the rest.

"Silver was special since she was born," Athena says. "I picked her out when she was just days old. She's true collie. She has a truly loving attitude, confidence, and intelligence."

Those qualities mean a lot to Athena.

"They are what allowed Silver to save my life," she says.

It was March 30, 1993. Athena, a diabetic, felt tired. She lay down on the bed in the basement to take a nap.

"I woke up with Silver pawing me, growling at me, and barking at me," Athena remembers. "I knew that something was wrong, because Silver never growls at me, and she never wakes me up."

Even as a nagging voice whispered that something was wrong, Athena was drifting back to sleep. But Silver wouldn't let her mistress rest. The dog stuck her nose under Athena's neck, trying to rouse her. She clawed at her, and barked again.

"I wasn't functioning well enough to know what was wrong at first," Athena says. "But somehow I realized I had to be low on blood sugar, because I couldn't think."

Athena's brain was functioning well enough for her to know that if she just lay there, she would die. She had to eat something.

"The only sugar in the house was upstairs," Athena says. "I tried to get off the bed, but I didn't have control of my limbs. I fell to the floor. I couldn't walk. I couldn't really even crawl."

Athena was so tired. All she really wanted to do, she says, was "curl up and go back to sleep." But Silver wouldn't let her.

"She kept harassing me until I started moving."

Athena began moving in a swimming/crawling motion across the floor toward the stairs. Every time she stopped, Silver would bark at her, shove her nose into her, and nip at her. Finally, after what seemed like hours, Athena made it to the bottom of the stairs. But she didn't know what to do next.

"I couldn't figure out how I was going to crawl up the stairs," she says.

Luckily, the stairs were open in the back. So, with Silver nudging her on, Athena grabbed hold of the first stair and pulled herself up. But her movements were so jerky that she fell against the nearest wall.

Don't let me bounce, she thought. But it was too late. She hit the wall on her left and bounced to the right. The staircase was wide and the other wall was far away. Athena knew she would fall on her side and then on her back. There was nothing to stop her. But then Silver came and put her left shoulder next to Athena's right side, keeping her mistress upright.

"If Silver hadn't been there I would have fallen down," Athena says. "And I was so uncoordinated, I wouldn't have been able to get myself back up very easily."

Athena grabbed the back of the next stair, bounced off the wall, and then off Silver again.

"We continued this way up to the top step,"

Athena says. "But there the wall I was bouncing against ended. And there was no way to grab on to the top step — it was just the floor."

Athena tried once to get up, but couldn't. So she tried desperately to get both of her arms around Silver's neck.

"She had to have confidence that I wasn't trying to hit her," Athena says, because of the way her arms were flailing around. "But she just stood there until I got both arms around her neck."

Once Athena got her arms around Silver, the 60-pound dog dragged her up the last step.

Athena then crawled toward the refrigerator. She knocked over a chair on the way with her jerky movements. But she made it to the refrigerator, from which she managed to extract a can of sweetened condensed milk. Silver sat beside her mistress while she drank the lifesaving fluid. Then Athena crawled to the phone and called 911.

"But of course I couldn't talk," Athena says. "I didn't have any coordination in my face. My facial muscles wouldn't move right." Athena was on the phone for some time before she managed to say the word, "Lassie." This conveyed the message that she lived at the house with all the collies, and the paramedics were on their way.

The milk worked quickly. With sugar in her bloodstream, Athena was starting to feel better when the paramedics arrived a short while later.

But the paramedics stayed a while anyway, to make sure that she was okay, and that she wasn't going to pass out again.

"Silver sat with me the whole time," Athena says. "She is an absolute sweetheart. I owe my life to her."

Tribber

Susan Pattman had to work long hours to pay for the show-quality boxer puppy she and her three-year-old son, Sean, had fallen in love with. "Is any dog worth this?" her husband, Mike, would often ask. He doesn't ask that question anymore. Tribber earned his keep, and then some, when he alerted Mike to a kitchen fire, helping to save Sean and the family's 100-year-old home.

As a volunteer at Jacquet's Boxers, Susan Pattman brought puppies to her Midland Park, New Jersey, home to socialize them. Once a puppy grew used to living with people, he would be sold — usually to someone who had already chosen him.

The 12-week-old boxer Susan brought home in September, 1992, was promised to a man in Brazil. Once the show-quality puppy had been socialized, he would be sent there, where his owner hoped he would be a champion in the ring.

This was the fifth puppy Susan had brought home to socialize, so she was totally unprepared for how she — and her toddler — felt about him.

"We just got especially attached to this dog," Susan says. And the feeling seemed to be mutual. "The dog saw Sean, and they became instant buddies," she says.

Susan wasn't sure what to do. She knew this dog was already promised to someone. And she also knew that show-quality boxers are very expensive — they cost more than she could ever afford. But she and Sean loved the dog.

Susan talked to Rick Tomita, the owner of the kennel. She asked if there was any way she could keep the dog.

Rick told her that he had other good dogs for the man in Brazil. And, since she did volunteer work there, he could give her a break on the dog's price. He could sell her the puppy for $1500.

Although considered a bargain for such a high-quality boxer, it was still more than Susan could afford. But she had to have the dog. So she and Rick worked out an arrangement whereby she would pay for the dog by working for Rick in the kennels.

Susan had to work a lot of hours to pay for the dog. So many, in fact, that her husband often wondered if she had made the right choice.

"Is any dog worth this?" he would ask.

Mike Pattman doesn't ask that question anymore. Not since the day in January 1993 that Tribber helped save Sean and the family's home during a fire.

Susan had left for school early that morning. While Sean watched a videotape, Mike went upstairs to do some work.

Sean decided he wanted a snack. Rather than bother his father, he decided to make it himself. He loaded the toaster oven with whatever he could find in the refrigerator, including a grapefruit. Then he pressed the "toast" button. He kept pressing the button until the oven started smoking.

Tribber, who had been keeping Sean company, knew that the smoke meant trouble. He ran upstairs to Mike's office and started barking. Mike thought the dog just wanted to go out and barely looked up from his work.

"I'll be with you in a minute," he told the dog.

Tribber returned just minutes later.

"Not now," Mike said.

But Tribber wouldn't take "no" for an answer. The 18-month-old dog took Mike's arm in his mouth and pulled his owner into the hall, where he could see the smoke. Then Tribber dashed down the stairs, with Mike close behind him.

Sean was still in the kitchen, watching the flames dance on the toaster oven and lick the wooden cabinet above it. Tribber grabbed Sean by his shirt and pants, then dragged the 30-pound boy out of the kitchen to safety.

Mike ran into the kitchen, grabbed the fire extinguisher, and put out the fire. Then, using hot pads to protect his hands, he carried the toaster oven outside, where the hot glass shattered in the extreme cold.

When Mike ran back in to see where Sean was, he found him in the dining room — under Tribber. The dog had lain down on top of Sean to keep him away from the fire.

When Mike saw what Tribber had done, he scratched his back and praised him.

"Good dog," Mike said. Tribber got up and released his charge.

Sean was frightened, but unharmed. And the damage to the 100-year-old wood-frame house was minimal. The Pattmans only had to replace the toaster oven and a kitchen cabinet. Susan's brother-in-law, a fire inspector, said it could have been a lot worse.

"All it would have taken is another couple of minutes for the whole kitchen to go," he told them. "Then a few minutes more and the whole upstairs."

The Pattmans had had a smoke detector, but when a pipe burst several weeks earlier and knocked down part of the ceiling, it took the smoke detector with it. Susan is now careful always to have a working smoke detector in the house — in addition to Tribber.

And no one in the family will ever again question paying $1500 for Tribber. The Pattmans know their dog — now a hero and a show champion — is priceless.

Willy

More than 1,000 people die each year as a result of carbon monoxide poisoning. In 1991, the odorless colorless gas might have counted one more among its victims if not for Willy. The nine-year-old weimaraner woke his owner just minutes before the gas would have taken her life.

Betty Souder of Los Alamos, New Mexico, remembers the night in January 1991 that Willy saved her life.

"I was sleeping soundly," she says, "when Willy came into my room and kept nudging me and nudging me, which was unusual. He sleeps in another room and usually if he wants to go out or something, he barks."

When Betty realized Willy wasn't going to leave her alone, she tried to rouse herself.

"I tried to get awake but couldn't seem to," she says. "But he kept at it. Finally, I sat up on the side of the bed. But I could hardly move. It was like I was drugged or something."

Betty finally managed to stand and then staggered down the hall to let Willy out. She felt so awful, she wondered if she'd had a stroke. But when Willy came back in, Betty noticed that he was staggering, too. That's when she realized they were both in trouble.

Since she had had a problem with the furnace in the past, she suspected carbon monoxide as the culprit. She managed to open a few windows to let in a little fresh air.

"Willy seemed to feel somewhat better," Betty says. "But I just got sicker and sicker."

Betty knew she needed help. She tried to call a friend who lived nearby, but every time she dialed the number, she dropped the phone. Finally, on her third try, her friend heard her.

"I just said, 'Oh, Kelly, help. I don't know what's wrong.' "

Betty knew they couldn't stay in the house any longer. She weaved back down the hall and out the door to the front porch to wait for her friend. Willy went with her.

Kelly came and took Betty and Willy straight to the hospital. A blood test showed that Betty had carbon monoxide poisoning.

"They said the carbon monoxide level in my

blood was really high," Betty says. "They had to give me seven hours of oxygen."

Probably because he was lower to the ground and didn't breathe as much poison, Willy was feeling much better than his mistress. He was feeling well enough, in fact, to enjoy the roast beef dinner that the hospital staff brought him in honor of his rescue.

"The doctor said a few more minutes and I probably never would have woken up," Betty says. "Willy probably didn't feel too well, but he just seemed to know he had to get me up."

Although Betty was grateful for her dog's actions, she wasn't at all surprised by them. When her husband was dying at home of a brain tumor several years earlier, Willy sat right beside him all the time. He seemed to know that his master was sick and needed a friend, Betty said.

"I know Willy is so fond of me and he was so fond of Dick that I do believe he would do anything for either of us. He's just been a wonderful pet."

Willy's lifesaving effort won him more than the praises of his mistress. It also won him a first-place tie in Ken-L Ration's 1991 Dog Hero of the Year contest.

Woodie

Rae Anne Knitter was waiting for her fiancé to return from taking a photo when her dog went crazy. Woodie tugged and pulled at her leash until Rae Anne let her go. Then the dog took off. Rae Anne followed her. When Woodie reached the edge of the cliff, she leapt off. Rae Anne stopped and looked down. Her fiancé was lying facedown in the river below. And Woodie was beside him, lifting his head so that he could breathe.

Ray Thomas brought his camera the Sunday morning in September 1979 that he, his fiancée, and her dog went hiking through the Cleveland Metroparks Rocky River Reservation. The amateur photographer hoped to capture some of the beauty of the fall day in that striking setting.

As they reached the top of a hill that overlooked a deep gorge cut by the river, Ray asked Rae Anne to hold Woodie back. He wanted to take some photographs and didn't want the dog running near the edge. Rae Anne held fast to Woodie's leash while Ray climbed out of sight.

Ray was standing in loose shale about 15 feet from the edge of the cliff, positioning himself for the shot, when something terrible happened.

"I was just about ready to take a picture when the area of ground that I was on gave out," he remembers. "It was all shale, and there was nothing to grab on to. I was sliding down. It was pretty steep."

Ray grabbed at his only hope.

"A tree was hanging out over the edge a little bit. . . . I got my left hand on it and swung. But before I could get my right hand on it, my left hand slipped off.

"I was just suspended in midair for a second," Ray says. "It was a strange feeling. Then I passed out."

Witnesses later told Ray that he then fell about 40 feet, bounced off a protrusion, fell another 40 feet or so, then rolled into the river, which was about three or four inches deep at that point. There he lay, facedown and motionless.

"I was lapsing in and out of consciousness," Ray says. "I couldn't lift my head. I could see that my hand was upside down so I knew that my arm had been broken." Ray didn't know that he had done more than break his arm. He had also crushed two vertebrae and pinched his spinal cord between the crushed bones.

Rae Anne didn't see Ray's fall. And, since Ray didn't scream, she didn't hear it, either. For all she knew, her fiancé was still at the cliff taking pictures. But Woodie knew differently.

"All of a sudden, Woodie just went crazy," Rae Anne later told Ray. "She just went nuts." The dog was pulling and tugging at her leash. Rae Anne couldn't figure out what it was, but she knew something was wrong. Her six-year-old dog never acted like this. Rae Anne let Woodie off her leash. The dog backed up about ten feet, then ran right off the cliff.

Like Ray, her fall wasn't a smooth one. The brave collie/shepherd dislocated her hips and crushed seven toes when she smashed into the protrusion where Ray broke his back and arm. But her injuries didn't slow her down.

"I heard a yelp and some stones falling," Ray says. "The next thing I knew, Woodie was nudging me, pulling my head out of the water so I could breathe. She did it real gentle. She didn't touch my arm. She knew something was wrong with it."

When Rae Anne looked down at this scene, she was terrified.

"I didn't know if he was dead or alive," she says of her fiancé. "He didn't move."

People on the other side of the river, who had witnessed the fall, shouted to Rae Anne to move back. They were afraid that she was going to panic and come tumbling down the cliff, too.

Rae Anne turned and ran down the other side of the hill and around to where Ray lay in the river. Several other people were already there, trying to help the wounded man and the dog.

An ambulance came and rushed Ray to the hospital. A stranger took Woodie to Rae Anne's mother's house so Mrs. Knitter could get her to the vet.

Doctors operated for six hours to remove the bone from Ray's spinal cord. It was one-and-a-half months before he could walk, and two months before he could leave the hospital.

Woodie's injuries were less severe. By the time Ray came home from the hospital, his rescuer was moving around "pretty good," Ray says, "just slow."

"She got big hugs and kisses the first time I saw her," Ray says. He and Rae Anne, who is now his wife, credit Woodie with saving Ray's life.

"There was a length of time when nobody was able to get to me," Ray says. "She just knew that something was up."

Woodie's bravery won her more than hugs and kisses. For her heroic rescue, Woodie was named Ken-L Ration's Dog Hero of 1980.